This Little Hippo
book belongs to

_____

_____

Scholastic Children's Books,
Commonvealth House, 1-19 New Oxford Street,
London WC1A 1NU, UK
a division of Scholastic Ltd

London • New York • Toronto • Sydney • Auckland

First published in 1998 in the UK by
Little Hippo, an imprint of Scholastic Ltd

Copyright ©Mike Dickinson 1998

ISBN 0 590 19988 9

Printed in Italy by Amadeus S.p.A.

2 4 6 8 10 9 7 5 3 1

The right of Mike Dickinson to be identified as the author
and illustrator of this work has been asserted by him in
accordance with the Copyright, Designs and Patents Act, 1988.

Danny's Picture

Mike Dickinson

One morning Danny woke up early.
It was a special day. It was his very
first day at school.

Mummy and the baby took him there.
"Now be a good boy, won't you, Danny?"
said Mummy as she waved goodbye.

Danny went into the classroom and sat down at his table.

He drew a picture of himself and wrote his name in big letters at the bottom.

Danny was very pleased with his picture.
It looked just like him. He showed the
picture to his teacher.

"Very good," she said. "It deserves a
gold star." The teacher pinned Danny's
picture on the classroom wall.

At break-time Danny went out into the
playground. He scared the school cat and
chased her up a tree.

The school caretaker climbed up
the tree and rescued her.
"Who frightened the cat?" he asked.
"Not me," smiled Danny.

In the classroom on the wall Danny's picture began to change. It looked a little bit different now.

At lunchtime, Danny sat next to Amanda.
He dropped a dried-up worm into her
custard when she wasn't looking.

When Amanda found the worm she
screamed and screamed. The dinner
lady had to clean up the mess.
"Who did that?" she said.
"It wasn't me," grinned Danny.

In the classroom on the wall Danny's picture changed again. It looked very different now.

When it was time to go home, Danny poured blue paint into one of Austin's wellington boots.

Austin put on his boot and the paint splashed everywhere.

Austin's mother was very cross.

"Who did that?" she said.

"Not me," smirked Danny.

In the classroom on the wall Danny's
picture changed again. It looked
completely different. Was it really Danny?

Mummy and the baby came to take
Danny home.

"What did you do at school today?"
asked Mummy.
Danny showed Mummy his picture.

When they got home, Danny's
Mummy looked at the picture again.
"What a horrid little monster!" said
Mummy and she stuck Danny's
picture on the fridge door.

At teatime somebody saved the cat
from the dog next door.

"Who saved the cat?" said Mummy.
"It was me," said Danny.

In the kitchen, on the fridge door,
Danny's picture began to change.

After tea someone gave the baby a ride
in their car.

"Ah," said Mummy, "Now who did that?"
"I did," said Danny. "I gave the baby a ride."

In the kitchen, on the fridge door, Danny's picture changed again.

At bedtime, someone put their pyjamas
on all by themselves.

"Who did that?" asked Mummy.

"It was me," smiled Danny.

In the kitchen, on the fridge door, Danny's picture looked just like Danny once more.

Grandma called in to say goodnight.
"What did Danny do at school today?"
asked Grandma.

"He drew a horrid little monster. I stuck
it on the fridge door," said Mummy.

When Grandma saw the picture she laughed. "That's not a horrid little monster," said Grandma. "It's Danny!"

"Danny's not a monster. He's a good boy, aren't you?" beamed Grandma.

"I will be tomorrow," said Danny.